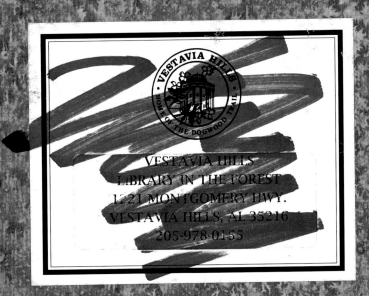

For Osky Bosky Boy (Oscar) — *M.P.R.*

First published in the United States 2001 by DIAL BOOKS FOR YOUNG READERS • A division of Penguin Young Readers Group • Published by The Penguin Group • Penguin Group (USA) Inc., 375 Hudson Street, New York, NY 10014, U.S.A. • Penguin Group (Canada), 90 Eglinton Avenue East, Suite 700, Toronto, Ontario, Canada M4P 2Y3 (a division of Pearson Penguin Canada Inc.) • Penguin Books Ltd, 80 Strand, London WC2R 0RL, England • Penguin Ireland, 25 St. Stephen's Green, Dublin 2, Ireland (a division of Penguin Books Ltd) • Penguin Group (Australia), 250 Camberwell Road, Camberwell, Victoria 3124, Australia (a division of Pearson Australia Group Pty Ltd) • Penguin Books India Pvt Ltd, 11 Community Centre, Panchsheel Park, New Delhi - 110 017, India • Penguin Group (NZ), Cnr Airborne and Rosedale Roads, Albany, Auckland 1310, New Zealand (a division of Pearson New Zealand Ltd) • Penguin Books (South Africa) (Pty) Ltd, 24 Sturdee Avenue, Rosebank, Johannesburg 2196, South Africa • Penguin Books Ltd, Registered Offices: 80 Strand, London WC2R 0RL, England

Published in Great Britain 2000 by Frances Lincoln Limited, 4 Torriano Mews, Torriano Avenue, London NW5 2RZ

The publisher does not have any control over and does not assume any responsibility for author or third-party websites or their content.
Manufactured in China on acid-free paper
10 9 8 7 6 5 4 3 2 1

Library of Congress Cataloging-in-Publication Data available upon request

The
EGG

M.P. Robertson

DIAL BOOKS FOR YOUNG READERS

George knew something wasn't right when he found more than he had bargained for under his mother's favorite chicken.

He moved the egg to the warmth
of his bedroom. For three days
and three nights he read the egg stories.

On the third night the egg started to rumble.

Something was hatching, and it definitely wasn't a chicken!

When the dragon saw George, it gave a chirrup of delight.

George didn't speak Dragon, but he knew exactly what the dragon had said:
"Mommy."

George had never been a mother before, but he knew that it was his motherly duty to teach the dragon dragony ways.

The first lesson he taught was *The Fine Art of Flying*.

The second lesson was *Fire and How to Breathe It*.

The third lesson was *How to Distress a Damsel*.

And the final lesson was *How to Defeat a Knight*.

Every evening, as all good
mothers should, George
read the dragon a bedtime
story.

One night, as he read
from a book of dragon
tales, the dragon looked
longingly at the pictures.
A sizzling tear rolled down
his scaly cheek.

The dragon was lonely.
He was missing his own kind.

The next morning the dragon had gone.
George was very sad. He thought he
would never see his dragon again.

But seven nights later he was woken
by the beating of wings. Excitedly
he pulled back the curtains. There, perched in
the tree, was the dragon. George opened
the window and clambered onto his back.

They soared into the night,
chasing the moon around
the world, over oceans and
mountains and cities.

Faster and faster they went,
until they came to a place that
was neither North nor South,
East nor West.

They swooped down through the clouds into a cave that gaped like a dragon's jaws. This was the place where dragons lived.

The dragon gave a roar of delight. He was home at last.

Finally it was time for George to leave.
Up, up they flew, chasing sleep through the night,
until they could see his home below.

George hugged his dragon tight,
and the dragon gave a roar. George
didn't speak Dragon, but he knew
exactly what the dragon had said:

"Thank you."